Another Fine Mess

One day while Sandy the fish was out for a morning swim, she heard a loud crash coming from inside the Little Mermaid's grotto. When she went to investigate, she found her brother Flounder throwing Ariel's things this way and that. "Flounder!" cried Sandy. "What are you doing?"

"I'm looking for Ariel's pearls," Flounder replied. "She said I could play marbles with them."

"Well, I hope you take better care of them than the seashells you borrowed from me the other day," Sandy said. "You lost three of my favorites and —"

© 1992 The Walt Disney Company

No portion of this book may be reproduced
without the written consent of The Walt Disney Company.

Produced by Kroha Associates, Inc.
Middletown, Connecticut

Illustrated by Yakovetic Productions

Written by M.C. Varley

Printed in the United States of America.

ISBN 1-56326-170-7

"Here they are!" Flounder shouted, interrupting his sister. He held the bag of pearls out for her to see. "These will make great marbles, don't you think?"

"What I think is that you should take better care of other people's things," Sandy said. "Just look at this mess! Why can't you put Ariel's things back where they belong?" But Flounder was so excited about finding the pearls he just swam away without hearing a word she'd said.

The little fish raced to his favorite play spot where the ocean floor was smooth and clear. He hurriedly pushed the other toys he'd left there to one side, poured Ariel's pearls out of the bag, and began to play. *If I can make a triple fludderblast,* he thought, carefully lining up the difficult shot, *I'll be the best marbles player in the whole world!*

But Flounder missed his shot. The pearl went sailing over a rock and hit poor Sebastian the crab smack in the back of the head!

"Ouch!" cried Sebastian, who had been enjoying a cozy nap. "That hurts!"

"So that's where it went!" Flounder said when he found Sebastian with the pearl. "I guess I hit it a little too hard."

"You certainly did," said the crab, rubbing his head. "Where did you get all those pearls, anyway?"

"Ariel let me borrow them," Flounder replied. "They make great marbles."

"Perhaps," said Sebastian, "but you really ought to be more careful. Remember what happened to that gold key I gave you to play with last week? You wouldn't want to lose Ariel's pearls, too."

"Don't worry," Flounder said. "I won't."

"And clean up after yourself when you're through," added the crab as he returned to his nap. "Your favorite playing spot looks as if it's been hit by a tidal wave!"

Just then a school of sea horses swam by. "Hi, Flounder!" one of them called out. "We're going to see who can swim the fastest from here to the old sunken ship. Want to join us?"

"That sounds like fun!" said Flounder. He raced off to join the others, forgetting all about Ariel's pearls, and about cleaning up his other toys.

Flounder easily won the race to the ship. "I win! I win!" he said, laughing. "Now let's play tag!"

The sea horses loved playing tag almost as much as Flounder did, and they were very good at it, too. Flounder was having such a good time that he completely forgot about Ariel's pearls.

When Ariel returned to her grotto she found Sandy cleaning up the mess Flounder had made. "What happened here?" asked the Little Mermaid.

"Flounder was looking for your pearls, and he forgot to clean up after himself," Sandy explained.

"That isn't all he forgot," said Ariel mysteriously as she put something into one of her many boxes. "And I think I know a way to teach him to be more responsible."

Meanwhile, Flounder was having a whale of a time playing with the sea horses. When they finished their game of tag they built all sorts of fancy sand castles under the sea, decorated with old shells and pretty colored coral.

"This is the most fun I've ever had!" laughed Flounder as he swam through one of the castle tunnels. "You sure know great places to play!" The sea horses even gave him some coral to take home when they were through playing.

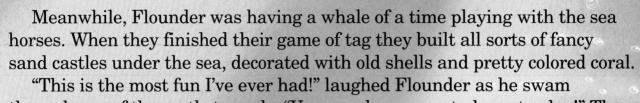

Flounder was so excited he couldn't wait to tell Sebastian about all the fun he'd had that day. "The sea horses even gave me some coral of my very own!" he said, showing Sebastian his present.

"That's very nice," replied Sebastian. "But I hope you remembered to put Ariel's pearls back before you went to play with the sea horses."

"Oops," said Flounder. "I forgot. I'll do it right now."

But when he went back to the place where he had been playing with the pearls, they were gone! *Oh, no!* he thought. *I've lost Ariel's pearls! What am I going to do?*

"There's only one thing you can do," said Sebastian when Flounder told him what had happened. "You have to tell Ariel the truth."

"I didn't mean to lose your pearls," Flounder said softly when he and Sebastian had reached the grotto. "It was an accident. I feel terrible about it and I'm very sorry."

Ariel saw that he really *was* sorry. "I have something to show you, Flounder," she said. "Look what I found today."

Ariel opened the box where the pearls were kept and pulled out a small bag. "The pearls!" cried Flounder. "They aren't lost after all!"

"You were very lucky this time," Ariel told him. "I found them lying on the ocean floor where you left them, but you really should be more careful when you borrow things. You already lost Sandy's favorite shells, and Sebastian's gold key."

"And I even lost the coral the sea horses just gave me!" Flounder said sadly, as he realized he had dropped it while looking for the pearls.

The next day, Flounder
decided to clean up his favorite
playing spot. He soon found Sebastian's gold key and Sandy's three favorite
shells. He even found his missing coral! Just then Sandy came swimming
around the corner. "Come on, Flounder!" she called out to him. "The sea
horses want us to play with them!"

"You go ahead!" Flounder called back. "I'll catch up with you later — first
I have to put all these things back where they belong!"